and inspired this story. I'd toast you with a glass of milk, but I can't drink the stuff.—K. W.

To Mom and Dad—M. H.

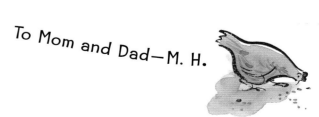

the cow loves cookies

by **karma wilson**

bestselling author of BEAR SNORES ON

illustrated by

marcellus hall

MARGARET K. McELDERRY BOOKS
New York London Toronto Sydney

MARGARET K. McELDERRY BOOKS

An imprint of Simon & Schuster Children's Publishing Division

1230 Avenue of the Americas, New York, New York 10020

For information about special discounts for bulk purchases, please contact Simon & Schuster

Special Sales at 1-866-506-1949 or business@simonandschuster.com.

The Simon & Schuster Speakers Bureau can bring authors to your live event. For more information

or to book an event, contact the Simon & Schuster Speakers Bureau at 1-866-248-3049 or visit

our website at www.simonspeakers.com.

Book edited by Emma D. Dryden

Book designed by Debra Sfetsios

The text for this book is set in Coop.

The illustrations for this book are rendered in ink and watercolor.

Manufactured in China

0410 SCP

10 9 8 7 6 5 4 3 2

Library of Congress Cataloging-in-Publication Data

Wilson, Karma.

The cow loves cookies / Karma Wilson ; illustrated by Marcellus Hall.—1st ed.

p. cm.

Summary: While all the other animals on the farm enjoy eating their regular food,

the cow chooses to eat the one thing that she loves best.

ISBN 978-1-4169-4206-1 (hc)

[1. Stories in rhyme. 2. Cows—Fiction. 3. Domestic animals—Fiction. 4. Farmers—Fiction.

5. Cookies—Fiction. 6. Humorous stories.] I. Hall, Marcellus, ill. II. Title.

PZ8.3.W6976Co 2010

[E]—dc22

2009000742

To Steve Malk, who also loves cookies

WHENEVER Farmer feeds the horse,

he feeds the horsey **hay,** of course.
The horse just loves to nibble hay.

He eats it
every single day.

But
the
cow
loves
cookies.

Farmer knows
what chickens
need.

He always gives them
chicken feed.

They **scratch** and **cluck** and **peck** all day.

They love their **feed.**

The horse loves **hay.**

But
**the
cow
loves
cookies.**

The farmer feeds
the geese each
morn.

He always gives
them sweet,
cracked **corn.**

They honk for joy and flap their wings.

Hay for horses,
yes indeed.

Give those chickens
chicken feed.

Corn for geese,
they love it so.

When Farmer
feeds the hogs
their slop,
they love to eat
that gooey glop.

They oink and snort;
they grunt with glee.

They eat like pigs,
it seems to me.

Of course,
we know the horse
loves **hay**.

And chickens love their
feed each day.

Geese love **corn**,
as all geese should.

The pigs
think **slop** is
mighty good.

But Cow would never eat that stuff.

You couldn't pay the cow enough!

Because . . .

the
cow
loves
cookies.

Farmer's dog just loves to eat when Farmer gives him **doggie treats.**

He gulps and gobbles
with **delight.**

He savors every meaty bite.

Hay is what the horsey needs.

The chickens all
eat **chicken feed.**

The geese munch **corn;**
it tastes so fine.

The hogs think **slop**

is just divine.

The dog adores his
doggy treats.

But Cow would rather
eat things sweet . . .

so
why
does
the
cow
love
cookies?

She and Farmer
made a deal,
and every day
they share a meal.

Farmer packs
a picnic lunch,
and when the two
sit down to munch,

he takes
cookies
from a tin

and Cow
gives **milk**
to dunk them in.

Cow is
happy.

Farmer
too.

They
both
LOVE
milk and cookies!

(But the duck loves **quackers**.)